MYSTERY OF THE FALLEN TREASURE

created by
GERTRUDE CHANDLER WARNER

ALBERT WHITMAN & Company
Chicago, Illinois

Library of Congress Cataloging-in-Publication Data is
on file with the publisher.

ISBN 978-0-8075-5508-8 (hardcover)
ISBN 978-0-8075-5506-4 (paperback)

Printed in the United States.
10 9 8 7 6 5 4 3 2 LB 18 17 16 15 14 13

Cover art copyright © 2013 by Tim Jessell.
Interior illustrations by Anthony VanArsdale.

For more information about Albert Whitman & Company,
visit our web site at www.albertwhitman.com.

Contents

MYSTERY OF THE FALLEN TREASURE

CHAPTER 1

A New Adventure

"Look, that plane is flying awfully low!" Six-year old Benny Alden pointed out the window of the minivan. A small plane glided down past the mountains and disappeared in the distance.

"It's landing at the little Sunriver Airport," said Grandfather. "Lots of people have small planes there."

"I bet that plane is too small to hold all of us and our suitcases," Benny's ten-year-old sister, Violet, said. "Especially since we also have Watch with us!" She petted the wire-haired dog that sat next to her.

The Aldens had landed at the airport just before noon and rented the mini-van. Grandfather's friend Victor Gonzales had invited the family to spend a week in beautiful Sunriver in central Oregon. They had traveled across the country from Greenfield, Connecticut.

"Dogs are welcome in Sunriver," said Henry, Benny and Violet's older brother. He was reading from a brochure that he had downloaded from the Internet. Henry was fourteen and liked to look things up on the computer. "It says that dogs just have to be on a leash or be very well behaved."

Twelve-year-old Jessie reached past Violet to pet Watch. He turned to nuzzle her hand. "Watch is very well behaved, aren't you, Watch?"

Watch was really Jessie's dog, but Jessie was happy to share him with her sister and brothers. Jessie had found Watch in the woods. When their parents died, Jessie,

Violet, Henry, and Benny had run away. They were supposed to live with their grandfather whom they had never met. They had heard that he was mean so they decided to hide from him. They discovered an abandoned boxcar in the woods and made it their home, which they shared with Watch. Their grandfather found them and they learned that he was not mean at all, but kind and loving. The Aldens became a family and Grandfather moved them all to his home in Greenfield. The boxcar was set up in the yard so the children could play there anytime they liked.

"The brochure also says that we can see the foothills of the Cascades from here," said Henry. "We are surrounded by wooded hills, mountains, and lakes."

Henry and the other children looked out the window at the scenery that surrounded them.

"What's a foothill?" asked Benny.

"It's a low hill at the base of a mountain or a mountain range," said Henry.

"They don't look like feet to me," said Benny.

Violet and Jessie laughed. "I bet they're called foothills because they are fun to walk on!" suggested Violet.

"That could be, Violet," said Henry. "Foothills are easier to hike up than mountains!"

"I hope we'll go hiking!" said Benny.

"I'm sure we will," said Jessie. "Watch will make sure that we do!"

"Grandfather, you'll want to turn right at the next street," Henry said. "Mr. Gonzales's house is just a few blocks away."

"Did you Google it on your cell phone?" Grandfather asked.

"Yes, I did," said Henry. The other children giggled. They knew that Henry loved high-tech devices.

They passed a small village with shops and restaurants and turned right.

"Are we there yet?" asked Benny. "I'm hungry—it must be past lunchtime!"

"We'll eat soon," promised Jessie. "We need to get our things put away first."

Grandfather steered the minivan into a circular driveway and pulled up next to a large log cabin. A woman waved at them from the front door and walked to the van as everyone got out. She had dark, curly hair and a friendly face.

"Greetings, Aldens!" she said as she helped grab suitcases.

"Oh my goodness, Marianella, you have grown up," said Grandfather. "Children, this is Victor's daughter, Marianella." Mr. Alden introduced Henry, Jessie, Violet, and Benny.

"We're pleased to meet you, Marianella," said Henry. The children all shook her hand.

"We're pleased to have you stay with us," said Marianella.

Watch sniffed at Marianella's hand and wagged his tail. "And this is Watch!" said Benny. "He smells something good on your hand."

"That's what he does when he thinks we have a treat for him," said Violet.

"That's funny and very smart of Watch," said Marianella. "Actually my father and I were just preparing lunch for everyone. Watch probably smells beef stew and cornbread!"

"Oooh! I love beef stew!" cried Benny. "And cornbread too."

"You love all food," laughed Jessie.

"I'll say hello to Victor," said Grandfather. He headed into the house.

Just then a huge brown-and-black dog charged up and sniffed excitedly at the Aldens.

"Goyo, how did you get loose?" asked Marianella. The dog ran to her side. "Don't worry, he is very friendly."

"We're very glad to meet you, Goyo," said Jessie. "Watch is also very friendly!"

Watch and Goyo sniffed noses and wagged their tails.

"I think lunch is ready," said Marianella. "Let's head inside and eat."

Benny was the first through the door. The rest of the family and Marianella carried in the baggage. After lunch the children helped wash and put away the dishes. Then Marianella showed them their room.

The large guest room had four bunk beds and plenty of space. The children put down the blankets they had brought from home for Watch. The dog settled on the blankets and Goyo joined him.

"This is almost like our boxcar," said Violet.

"Only this has real bunk beds instead of pine needle beds," said Benny.

Violet was looking at the photos on the wall. "Who is this?" she asked.

"Those are pictures of my sister, Adelita," said Marianella. "She's an airplane pilot."

"Wow, that's exciting," said Henry. "I would love to learn how to fly an airplane."

"Yes, Adelita has always been the adventurous one," said Marianella. She studied the photos and sighed. "Father and I never know what she will do next. She has been acting strange lately."

Just then Goyo hopped up and came over to lick Marianella's hand. "Oh, you smart boy," she said, ruffling his head. "It's almost time to go, isn't it?"

"Where are you and Goyo going?" Benny asked.

"Oh, Benny, you're so nosy!" said Violet.

"It's okay," said Marianella. "We have a search-and-rescue training session in the foothills this afternoon."

"Goyo is a search-and-rescue dog?" Henry asked. "I've read about how dogs help find victims of disasters like earthquakes and avalanches. It sounds like dangerous work."

"It can be dangerous work, Henry," said Marianella. "And most SAR teams—as we're called—don't do it for money or glory."

"Wow," said Violet. "Have you and Goyo ever saved someone?"

"Goyo and I mostly look for lost hikers," said Marianella. "Sadly a lot of people get lost in this area. Some people don't tell anyone where they're going, and often they aren't prepared for an emergency. We have to act fast."

"If Goyo already knows how to search, how come you still practice?" Benny asked. He was eye level with the big dog. Goyo slipped over and licked Benny's face.

"We never stop practicing and training," said Marianella. "SAR requires handlers and their dogs to be in tip-top shape." Watch sniffed at Marianella and she bent down to pet him. "Say, let's see what kind of search dog Watch might be. If he can sniff out beef stew and cornbread, I bet he can sniff out a lost hiker!"

Marianella and the children headed to the huge, fenced-in backyard. "Okay, here's what we'll do," said Marianella. "Jessie and Violet can hold Watch and cover his eyes while Henry and I hide Benny."

Jessie and Violet carefully covered Watch's eyes with Violet's scarf as Marianella, Henry, and Benny raced to the end of the yard and disappeared around the corner of a shed. Henry and Marianella returned without Benny.

"Okay, Benny is ready," said Marianella. "Watch already knows his scent, so just tell him to find Benny."

"Watch, find Benny!" said Jessie. She followed Watch as he ran around the yard. He sniffed the ground and sometimes stopped to sniff the air. He looked back at Jessie after a few minutes. "I think Watch is confused," said Jessie.

"Just encourage him," said Marianella. "Tell him to find Benny. Dogs often need encouragement to keep searching."

"Find Benny!" said Jessie. "You can do it! I know you can!" Watch circled back around the yard then stopped and sniffed again. He suddenly yipped and ran around the shed with Jessie following. He stopped at a truck that was parked there. Watch jumped up on the tailgate and barked.

"You found me!" yelled Benny as he stood up. The other children and Marianella joined them and helped Benny out of the truck bed.

"Watch did great, didn't he?" Benny said as he hugged the dog close. The other children also petted and praised Watch.

"Yes, Watch did very well," said Marianella. "Hey, would you all like to come with me?" Marianella looked at the children crowded around their dog.

"To a real search-and-rescue training session?" Henry asked.

"Yes, you will be my special guests," said Marianella. "You can work with Watch on some object-searching skills. Plus we can always use new bodies to hide. Benny is a champ at playing the part of a lost hiker."

"As long as you don't forget where you hide me," said Benny.

"Who can forget you?" laughed Jessie. "You always make your presence known."

"Then it's settled. Let's go," said Marianella.

"This will be fun," said Violet. "I'll bring my camera. Maybe Watch will find something exciting!"

Marianella and the Alden children drove out of Sunriver and into the Cascade foothills close by. Marianella parked her jeep in a gravel parking lot surrounded by woods.

Benny noticed a bumper sticker on the back window of the jeep. "*SAR means search and rescue!*" he read aloud. Benny was just learning to read. He liked to try to read signs everywhere he went.

"That's right, Benny," said Marianella. She led the children to a trail into the woods. "Hey, we're here and I brought some help!" she called.

"Over here," said a voice. They all walked over to a campsite where a man and a dog were standing. Marianella introduced the Alden children to Jason and his dog, Bounce.

"This is our dog, Watch," said Jessie. "He is just learning about search and rescue."

"And I know how to get lost!" added Benny.

Everyone laughed. Watch was off his leash and running around in the woods. Suddenly he started barking.

"What's the matter with Watch?" Benny asked.

"We need to go see!" said Jessie.

The children ran to catch up with their dog. Watch was standing in a small clearing and wagging his tail. A bright yellow backpack lay in front of him. It was muddy and partly open.

"It looks like a backpack, but what's inside?" asked Violet. Something in the backpack was glinting in the sun that streamed through the trees.

The children praised Watch and approached the bright yellow backpack carefully. Henry picked up a stick and poked at it then peered inside. Violet was right behind him. Her brown eyes opened wide when she saw the contents.

"It's filled with jewelry!" she cried. "Beautiful jewelry!"

CHAPTER 2

A Find!

Violet loved art objects, especially things that were purple or blue. Jessie and Benny joined Violet and Henry to inspect the glinting gold and gemstone jewelry.

Violet carefully tipped the backpack so that they could see more of the contents. Inside were boxes of different sizes. Many of the boxes had come open. A tangle of gold necklaces, bracelets, and earrings lay in a jumbled mess.

"It looks like someone dropped this

backpack and kept going," said Henry.

"Oh my! Maybe it was stolen," said Jessie. "Violet, maybe you could take photos. Then we'll have a record to show the owner."

"Good idea," said Henry. "We can show what the backpack looked like when we found it."

"And it's so pretty!" Violet said. She snapped a few photos with her digital camera. Henry and Jessie looked inside the backpack for clues to its owner.

"Here's a piece of paper," said Jessie.

"What does it say?" asked Henry.

"*Twila's Handcrafted Jewelry Creations in Sunriver Village* is in fancy writing across the top," said Jessie. Benny stretched to look at the paper while Jessie continued to read. "*Dear Mr. Anderson, thank you for your payment of five thousand dollars. Here is the jewelry that you chose for your store in Portland. Each piece is one of a kind. I hope that your customers are pleased with your choices.*"

"Wow, that's a lot of money!" Henry exclaimed. He zipped the backpack closed

and strapped it to his back. "We should take this to Twila's Handcrafted Jewelry Creations right away!"

Just then Watch barked and ran toward the woods that surrounded the clearing. He stopped at the trees and wagged his tail.

"Look, someone's there," said Jessie. A figure appeared between the trees and then disappeared deeper into the woods.

"Maybe it was Jason or Marianella looking for us," Henry said. "We need to tell them about Watch's find."

* * *

"Here you are!" said Marianella when the children returned to the campsite.

"We thought we were going to have to search for you guys!" said Jason.

He noticed the yellow backpack that Henry had strapped to his back. "Where did that come from?"

Henry removed the backpack and showed Marianella and Jason what was inside. "Watch found this in the woods. It looks like it was dropped."

Jason and Marianella admired the tangle of jewelry.

"I wonder how this backpack wound up in the woods," said Jason.

"Maybe it fell from the sky!" Benny said.

"Oh, Benny, jewelry doesn't fall from the sky," said Violet. "Jessie and Henry think that somebody stole it then dropped it for some reason."

"We found a letter inside the backpack," said Jessie. "It's from Twila's Handcrafted Jewelry Creations in Sunriver Village."

"I know the store and Twila very well," said Jason. "She's a jewelry maker. Twila and I studied silver jewelry making at the same school."

Jason leaned over Benny and looked closely at the jewelry in the backpack.

Violet observed the jewelry that Jason was wearing—a watch with a gold, coral, and turquoise band, and multiple gold rings. She noticed he had a pierced ear but was not wearing an earring.

"Do you sell handmade jewelry too?" Violet asked Jason.

"Oh, some," said Jason. "But I could never afford to have my own jewelry store like Twila." He frowned.

"We also saw someone running in the woods," said Henry. "We thought it might be one of you."

"I was here with Goyo, working on our training schedule," said Marianella.

"I had Bounce down by the river," said Jason. "I wonder who it might have been."

"Maybe it was the thief!" said Jessie. "We need to take the backpack to Twila."

"Yes," said Marianella. "If it was stolen, I'm sure that she will want to contact the police."

"All right," said Jason. "I'll see you tomorrow, Marianella."

"See you later, Jason," said Marianella. "Come on, Aldens, let's head back to Sunriver. We need to return this backpack to Twila right away."

CHAPTER 3

Twila's Handcrafted Jewelry Creations

Goyo and Watch collapsed in the back of the jeep and slept during the drive back to Sunriver. Jessie reached back and petted both dogs.

"They must be tired from all that searching," she said.

"You bet," said Marianella, "and hungry too. I'll give them food and water when we get to Twila's store."

Marianella guided the jeep through the little community and pulled up to Twila's store. Henry grabbed the yellow backpack and got out of the jeep with Jessie, Violet, and Benny.

The store was across the street from a large park. Henry noticed that it had a nice view of the foothills from the front window. The Aldens entered the store, and a bell on the door jingled. Jessie noticed a pair of binoculars sitting on a table by the big front window.

Inside, a woman wearing a visor on a head of frizzy blond hair was bent over a worktable behind a long display counter. The children waited quietly while the woman worked. She opened the dome lid of a small, boxy machine and pulled out a bowl. They watched her carefully pour a mixture from the bowl into a little metal container. She put the container into the machine, shut the lid, and flipped a switch. Then she noticed the four children watching her.

"Oh my! You startled me," she said, standing and wiping her hands on her apron. "May I help you?"

"Oh, we're so sorry," Jessie said. "We didn't mean to scare you. We didn't want to disturb your work." Jessie introduced her brothers and sister.

"Are you Twila, the jewelry maker?" asked Violet.

"Yes, that's me," said Twila. "Is there something you want to buy from my store?" She looked at the four young children.

"Actually, we have something that we think belongs to you," Henry said. He held up the backpack so that Twila could see it.

"Oh my!" said Twila again. "Yes, that is my backpack. Where did you find it?"

"Our dog, Watch, found it in the foothills nearby," said Benny. "He is a search-and-rescue dog!"

"Give it to me," Twila said sharply. She came around the counter and reached for the backpack as Jessie handed it to her.

"Look at this muddy mess," Twila muttered, holding up the backpack. "This is why I like brown suitcases. They don't show dirt."

"I like bright yellow," said Violet. "It makes me feel sunny even when it's raining outside."

"I never thought anything could get this dirty! Yellow is very hard to get clean," griped Twila. "I never buy anything yellow. This backpack is ruined."

"We wondered how the backpack ended up in the woods," Jessie said. "Did someone steal it from you?"

"I don't know," said Twila. "I hired a pilot

named Adelita from the Sunriver Airport. She was supposed to deliver the backpack to my customer in Portland. But my customer called a little while ago and said that Adelita has still not shown up. I called and left Adelita a message, but she hasn't called back. I was just about to call her again."

"Oh no," said Jessie. "Adelita is Marianella's sister! What if Adelita's plane crashed? We should go to the airport right away and find out!"

"I'll be right behind you," said Twila. "I would like to know how my jewelry wound up in the woods. Adelita has some explaining to do."

The children hurried to tell Marianella what they had learned.

"I hope Adelita is okay," said Marianella as the Aldens piled into the jeep. "She seems to get in all kinds of trouble, but this is scary." Marianella drove quickly toward the airport.

"Did you notice the binoculars on the counter?" Jessie asked her brothers and sister.

"Yes, I did. That was strange," said Henry. "Jewelers use magnifying glasses to see close-up, not binoculars that see things far away."

* * *

A small plane lifted from the runway and looped back over Sunriver Village just as Marianella steered the jeep into the airport parking lot.

"That must be the way the planes head out," said Henry.

"Adelita's plane should be parked by the hangars," said Marianella. "I'm not sure where, and it looks like nobody is around."

"What's a hangar?" Benny asked as they walked quickly past a row of metal buildings.

"These metal buildings are hangars," said Henry. "Airplanes can be parked inside them."

"That's Adelita's plane at the end!" Marianella cried. She and Goyo raced down the row of airplanes.

Watch tugged on his leash as the children rushed to follow Marianella.

"What's up with you, Watch?" Jessie asked.

"He's acting like he found something," Benny said. "Maybe we should let him go."

"Good idea, Benny," said Henry. "Watch is a search dog, after all!"

Jessie detached the leash and Watch took off down the row of planes. He stopped in front of a small plane parked in front of a hangar. The children caught up as he sniffed at a door on the side of the airplane, wagging his tail. Marianella was peeking inside the windows.

"I'm so relieved!" said Marianella. "But where is Adelita? What kind of trouble is she in now?" She shook her head sadly.

"I think Watch may have a clue," said Jessie. "What do you smell, Watch?"

"That's funny—the door he's sniffing is open," said Violet.

Benny reached up and felt the bottom edge of the door. It felt sticky! He started to say something but was interrupted.

"What are you doing here?" A tall man wearing a tan shirt and blue jeans stood at the hangar door. "Get away from that plane!" he yelled.

CHAPTER 4

High in the Sky

"Hello, Rick," said Marianella calmly. "We're looking for my sister Adelita. Have you seen her today?"

Rick looked at the group that surrounded Adelita's airplane. "Adelita isn't here. Why are you looking for her, Marianella?" he asked. "And who are these children?"

Henry introduced himself and his brother and sisters. "We found a backpack full of jewelry that Adelita was hired to fly to Portland today," he said. "We found the backpack in the foothills. We wanted to ask Adelita what happened."

"Do you think Adelita stole the jewelry?" asked Rick. "If that's what you think, you are wrong. Adelita is a good friend of mine. I know she is not a thief."

Jessie noticed that Rick was fidgeting. "Do you know where she is?" she asked him.

"Adelita left for Portland this morning," said Rick. "She got back while I was away. I have no idea where she went after she parked her plane. I've left her several messages but she hasn't returned my calls." Rick sighed. Jessie realized that he must have been very worried.

"Do you mind if we look around the hangar?" Henry asked. "There might be a clue in there."

"Sure," said Rick. "Anything to help find Adelita and prove that she is not a thief."

Rick watched as Marianella and the children looked around the space where Adelita kept her things.

"Adelita loves to camp, as you can see by the photos on the wall," said Marianella.

"She also loves butterscotch candy," said Rick. He pointed to a big bowl of yellow candy on a wooden trunk by the wall. Henry spied a pair of leather gloves lying next to the bowl of candy.

The children looked at the photos. One showed Adelita standing by a tent. She had long blond hair in a ponytail and a big smile. In another photo she stood by an airplane with a grin and both thumbs up.

"That photo was taken after she got her license to fly last year," Rick said. "Adelita worked very hard for it. I just know she wouldn't risk it all over some jewelry."

"Then where is she?" Henry asked.

"That's what I would like to know!" Twila marched through the open doorway of the hangar. "I just discovered that a very special necklace is missing from this backpack!" Twila held up the yellow backpack, which she'd brought with her. "The necklace is one of a kind."

"Did you look all through the backpack?" asked Violet. "Things looked pretty jumbled up inside."

"Yes, I stood outside and went through everything while you were chatting," said Twila, obviously upset. "I packed the backpack myself and the necklace was right on top in a special box. It was my favorite creation. I didn't want to sell it, but I needed the money and the customer from Portland wanted to buy it."

"We're very sorry," said Henry. "You have everything that we found. But we could go back to the woods and look some more..."

Twila glared at the children. "You do whatever you like. I need to call the police now. It looks like Adelita stole the piece and tried to hide the rest in the woods."

Twila seemed to notice Rick for the first time. "You're her friend, aren't you? I've seen you and Adelita in my store, though you never bought anything."

"I tried to buy something, but you told me that it wasn't for sale," said Rick. "Heck of a way to do business."

"I have plenty of items for sale!" snapped Twila. "Maybe you were just checking out the goods that you and Adelita planned to steal."

"Adelita is no thief," said Rick. "And neither am I." He frowned at Twila.

Twila turned and stormed outside the hangar. Henry heard Twila's cell phone ring and overhead her say, "Thanks for calling. Yes, it was insured. I would like to file a claim."

"Whew," said Rick. "Twila is really mad. I hope I find Adelita before she does!"

"Where do you think Adelita might be?" asked Jessie.

"I don't know, but I think she must be okay since her airplane is here," said Rick. "I want to help find her, but right now I have to fly to Redmond." He noticed Henry's eyes open wide. "Say, how would you kids like to come along? It will take only about an hour," Rick said.

"In one of these little planes?" Benny asked. "Will we all fit?"

"No problem," said Rick. "We can even take Watch. I have a travel harness for dogs."

"Watch had to ride inside a kennel in the baggage compartment on the way to Oregon," said Jessie. "He'll like having a window seat this time!"

"You guys have fun," said Marianella. "I'm going to check Adelita's apartment. I'll see you at the house later." The children waved good-bye as Marianella and Goyo left to look for Adelita.

"Okay, let's go," said Rick. He led the children to the plane parked next to Adelita's. Benny looked at the baggage door on Adelita's plane again but didn't say anything. Rick opened the double doors to his plane, and the children and Watch climbed in. Rick helped the children buckle up. He and Jessie put a travel harness on Watch and attached it to the seat belt. Watch kept licking their hands.

"Watch is very excited," said Violet. "He is ready for action!"

Rick got into the pilot's seat and called ahead to the Redmond airport. Henry sat next to Rick and looked at the controls in front of him.

"You can be my copilot, okay, partner?" asked Rick.

Henry nodded.

"I think he's speechless," Jessie whispered to Violet and Benny. They giggled and held tight to one another's hands as the plane headed down the runway and took to the air. The little plane jumped and bucked in the sky.

"This is fun!" yelled Benny. "It's like a carnival ride."

"I'm glad you're having fun, Benny," said Violet unhappily. "This is like riding a bucking horse!"

"That is turbulence," said Jessie. "You'll get used to it. Just hang on and take deep breaths." Jessie patted her little sister's hand.

"We'll be flying pretty low so you'll see a lot of interesting things," said Rick. "Look at that herd of mountain goats down there."

Benny stuck his nose up against the window. "They look like furry white toys!" he said.

The children leaned close to the windows as the little plane passed over Sunriver,

banked, and headed across the foothills. Watch seemed to be interested in looking out the window too. The jumpy, bumpy ride didn't seem to bother him at all.

"Hey, look at that," said Violet. She felt a little calmer now that they were higher up. "There's a big clearing down there. Is that where Watch found the yellow backpack?"

"Maybe so," said Henry, who finally found his voice. "I think I saw the little gravel parking lot where we parked."

"Hey, I see someone down there!" said Benny.

"So do I," said Violet. "Wearing a bright red jacket and waving up at us!"

"I wonder who it is," Jessie said. "Why would that person wave at us?"

"It's probably just a hiker being friendly," said Rick. "Hey, look up there, on the left, that's Mount Bachelor. Isn't it beautiful?"

Jessie, Violet, and Benny admired the snowy mountain in the distance. Henry noticed that Rick was trying to distract them from the person in the clearing.

Soon Rick landed at the airport in Redmond. He asked the Aldens to sit tight for a few minutes. He opened a door in the nose of the plane and took out a large box. An airport worker loaded the box into a baggage carrier and drove toward the terminal. Rick slammed the door shut, latched it, and got back into the plane. He called to get the okay to enter the runway.

"Are you a flying mailman?" Benny asked.

Rick laughed. "Not exactly. I do all kinds of errands for people and businesses. That was a package of supplies for a local hospital."

"Was the box in a baggage compartment?" asked Violet. She remembered the open door on Adelita's plane.

"It's one of them," said Rick. "There is another baggage compartment in the back of the plane. But the one up front holds quite a bit."

Rick was next to take off, so the children held hands again as the little plane raced along the runway and lifted into the air. They circled back toward Sunriver and landed a short time later. They didn't pass over the clearing this time.

Rick taxied the little plane to its spot next to Adelita's plane. He and Henry helped unbuckle Jessie, Violet, Benny, and Watch.

"That was fun!" said Benny. "More fun than a carnival ride!"

"Yes, it was very fun," said Violet. "Thank you for taking us for a ride in your plane."

"Thanks for letting Watch go too," said Jessie. "He has had a lot of adventures today."

"You're welcome," said Rick. "I transport SAR teams all the time. I don't mind the dog hair on the seats!" He laughed then became serious. "I'll let you know if I talk to Adelita. We need to solve this mystery."

"Don't worry, we will," said Benny. "We love to solve mysteries!"

The children walked Watch back to Victor's house. "Did you notice how Rick changed the subject from the person in the red jacket who waved at us?" Jessie asked.

"Yes, and then he took a different route

to come back to Sunriver," Henry noted. "I think he knew who it was."

"I think we do too," said Jessie. "It was Adelita."

CHAPTER 5

The Missing Pilot

Early the next morning Marianella had a phone message from Adelita.

"She said she's okay, just out backpacking in the mountains," Marianella told the children. "It's what she loves to do, but when I asked her about the backpack, she said she would tell me later."

Victor and Marianella were relieved but still worried. They didn't like that Twila was accusing Adelita of being a thief. But Adelita hadn't told them what had happened to the backpack.

40

"We should take Watch back to the foothills to see if we can find more clues," said Henry. "Maybe we can find Adelita and talk to her."

"That's a great idea," said Marianella. "Jason and I were going to do some more practice sessions today. I can give you a ride up there."

"How about breakfast first?" asked Jessie.

"Sounds good to me!" said Benny.

Jessie loved to cook. She found the ingredients in the big country kitchen to create walnut pancakes. Violet made freshly squeezed orange juice. Benny poured glasses of milk for everyone with a little help from Henry.

"My grandchildren love to help whenever they can," said Grandfather as he joined them all at the big table.

"It's my pleasure to have someone else cook for a change!" said Victor.

Marianella laughed. "I am terrible at cooking, so Father does it all. But I do have other talents!"

Victor took her hand and smiled. "I know, and I'm very proud of the search-and-rescue work that you do. Both you and Adelita are very adventurous women."

"And I'm proud of these children and Watch," said Marianella. "They have a real knack for searching!"

Henry and Benny picked up the breakfast dishes and everyone pitched in to clean up.

The Aldens packed bottled water and leftover pancakes into their daypacks. Jessie made sure they had a first aid kit. Henry had charged his cell phone overnight and checked that it was working. They gathered their jackets and were ready to go. Watch tugged at his leash as Jessie loaded him into Marianella's jeep.

Marianella drove the children to the foothills. "We'll meet you at the base camp in a couple of hours," she said. "I hope you can find clues that Adelita is innocent."

The children said good-bye and put on their daypacks. They hiked to the woods where Watch had found the yellow backpack the day before. If Adelita had been there earlier, they might find a trail to follow. Henry pulled out a glove from his pocket and showed it to his brother and sisters.

"That glove was on top of Adelita's trunk in the hangar!" said Violet.

"Yes, it was," said Henry. "I'll return it, but I wanted something for Watch to sniff."

"That way he'll know the smell of the person we want him to find," said Benny.

"That's a good idea," said Jessie. "You always have a good plan, Henry!"

Henry let Watch sniff the glove then said, "Find her, Watch!"

"You can do it, Watch!" added Benny.

Jessie let Watch off his leash. He weaved back and forth around the clearing. Then suddenly he bolted into the woods. The children followed. Once in a while, Watch stopped and sniffed. Then he took off running again.

"Watch sure is acting like he smells something!" Violet said. "I can hardly keep up!"

"He's stopped up ahead," said Jessie. "He's looking back at us."

"Look," said Benny. "It's a campsite."

The children made their way through the brush and trees and found themselves standing in another small clearing. Watch sniffed around the remains of a campfire. He looked at Jessie and wagged his tail.

"I think Adelita was here," said Jessie. "I don't think Watch would care if it was someone else."

"We'll need to look around for more clues," said Henry. "Watch is a great search dog, but he is new at it!"

The children searched all around the campsite. They noticed an indentation in the grass.

"I think someone slept here," said Jessie. "It's close to the campfire and the right size to be a person.

Henry carefully touched the bottom of the campfire pit. "The campfire pit is cold and wet," he said. "Someone recently doused it with water."

Violet peered into a trash bin nearby. "I found something!" she cried. She handed a wad of cellophane to Benny.

"Hey, look, yellow candy wrappers!" he cried.

"Butterscotch. The same kind that Adelita loves," said Jessie. "She was here all right."

"If she hid the backpack in the clearing after stealing the necklace, why would she camp here?" Henry asked. He thought for a minute. "I agree with Rick. Adelita must be innocent."

"Then why was she here?" asked Jessie.

"Maybe she is hiding," said Henry. "Let's keep looking for her. If Adelita spent the night here, she can't be far away."

Jessie let Watch sniff the glove again. "Find her, Watch!" she said. Watch raced from the campsite and back into the woods. "We should have a search grid set up," said Jessie. "Then we wouldn't cover the same area over and over." She puffed to catch her breath.

"I think Watch has his own searching method," Henry said, laughing. "We just have to keep up with him!"

The four children followed Watch as he ventured down a hill and onto a worn footpath.

"Whew, at least it will be easier to follow him now," said Violet. "I was getting tired!"

"Me too," said Benny.

"Let's rest for a few minutes," said Jessie.

The children agreed to take a break. Jessie called Watch, who quickly came and lay down by her side.

"I think Watch is a little tired too," said Violet.

The children sat alongside the path, munching on pancakes and drinking the water they had packed. Henry poured water from his bottle into a bowl that he had brought along for Watch.

"I feel like we're back in the woods at our boxcar," said Violet.

"That was fun, wasn't it?" said Jessie. "Henry brought us loaves of bread, and we divided a loaf among us."

"And we gave some to Watch," Benny reminded her.

"That's right!" Jessie broke off a piece of her pancake and gave it Watch. He gobbled it down and lapped up more water. "You usually don't get people food, but this will be an exception," said Jessie.

Watch licked his lips.

"Is everyone ready to start searching again?" Henry asked.

"I'm always ready!" said Benny. Violet and Jessie smiled and said they were ready too.

"Let's go find Adelita, Watch!" said Henry.

Watch took off again but wasn't gone for very long. He came bounding back down the path toward Jessie, barking and wagging his tail.

"Look, Watch is already back," called Jessie. "He's acting like he found something."

Watch wagged his tail some more. Then he yipped and ran back up the path. The children followed as Watch turned and bounced into the woods.

"I hear someone talking," said Benny.

"Shh!" said Henry. The children all stopped and listened. They heard a voice in the distance.

"Hey there, boy, where'd you come from?" asked the voice.

The children crept into the trees and peeked through the branches. A woman sat on a log by a large tree. Her feet were bare and her socks and muddy boots were close by. She had a red jacket tied around her waist.

"I'll bet that's Adelita," whispered Jessie. "She looks like her photo."

The Aldens waited quietly as the woman petted Watch and talked to him.

"It's very nice to see a friendly face," the woman said. "I'm afraid that I'm in terrible trouble. I've been here all night, looking for something I lost." She ruffled the fur on Watch's neck and nuzzled him. "It was a backpack full of valuable jewelry. I've been searching and searching."

Watch licked her face and the woman laughed.

"Maybe you can help me find it, old boy," she said. "I would appreciate it very much."

"So, she is innocent," Jessie whispered.

"That's right," whispered Violet. "Nobody would lie to a dog. People trust dogs."

"And dogs only like good people," said Benny.

Henry smiled. "Let's say hello to Adelita," he said.

Watch barked and wagged his tail as the children appeared from the woods. Adelita looked surprised, then smiled when Watch ran over to greet them.

"Hello there," she said and waved at the children. "Are we having a party in the woods?"

"Yes," said Henry. "We're having a search party for Adelita. Are you Adelita?"

"Yes, I am," said the woman. "Why are you searching for me?"

"Because we found your missing backpack!" blurted Violet. "It was filled with beautiful jewelry."

"Watch found it while we were practicing search and rescue," said Benny. "He's a very smart dog!"

"Oh, that's wonderful news!" cried Adelita.

"I've been looking everywhere for that backpack. I thought it was lost forever or that someone found it and took it. I was so upset when it went flying out of my airplane!"

CHAPTER 6

Coming Unhinged

"It fell out of your airplane?" asked Henry. "Well, that explains how it got out here. But how did it fall out?"

Adelita pulled on her socks and struggled with her muddy hiking boots. "I bought that plane from a pilot who retired," she explained. "It needed work, but I got a good deal. But the front baggage door would pop open in the air if we had turbulence."

"I know what turbulence is," said Benny. "It's like a carnival ride!"

"That's right," said Adelita. "A bumpy ride, like riding on a bucking horse in these hills. The door would fly open. Then I'd have to circle back to the airport and tape it shut. But tape didn't always work. I was featured in the Sunriver newspaper when I lost a load of piñatas that I was flying to Portland for a Cinco de Mayo celebration. The piñatas scattered all over town."

"Piñatas in the streets!" said Jessie. "That would be quite a news story!"

"And lots of candy for everyone," added Benny. He licked his lips.

Adelita smiled. Then she continued her story. "The door was finally fixed right, or so I thought. But then yesterday morning, it popped open over the foothills. I saw that yellow backpack go flying out. I tried to watch where it landed. Then I flew back to the airport, got my camping gear, and came back to look for it. I was here all night, searching."

"Watch found it in a big clearing," said Henry.

"I am so glad to hear that," said Adelita.

"I wanted to find the backpack before Twila knew it was missing. I noticed that Twila called my cell phone but I haven't called her back yet."

"Rick tried to reach you too," said Jessie.

Adelita hung her head. "I know, but I didn't want him to get in trouble too. I waved at him when I saw his plane fly over yesterday so he knows I'm okay. You see, Rick is the one who fixed the door for me. He would feel like it was his fault that it came open again."

"We saw you," said Benny. "We were in the plane with Rick."

"I'm glad you met Rick," said Adelita. "He's a good guy."

"Did you say that Rick fixed the door?" Henry asked.

"That's right," said Adelita. "He knew I was taking valuable cargo this time so he worked on the door the night before. He put in all new parts." Adelita sighed. "Well, at least the backpack has been found. I'm so grateful to you all and to Watch!"

Jessie and Violet looked at each other. Jessie

could tell that Violet didn't want Adelita to know the bad news. But somebody had to tell her.

Adelita looked at their troubled faces. "What is it? What aren't you telling me? Is Rick all right?"

"Rick is okay," Henry assured her. "But Twila is not okay. She noticed that a very special necklace was missing from her backpack. She's very upset about it."

"Oh no!" Adelita cried. "Twila was very careful about packing that necklace into the backpack after she showed it to me." Adelita explained how Twila insisted on putting her backpack into the front baggage compartment by herself. The pack was zipped up tight. "She knew about the problems I'd had. She said that she wanted to secure the door herself. I didn't mind. I was inside getting my plane ready for takeoff."

"We noticed the door was open when we looked at your plane at the airport," Henry said.

"I didn't take the time to look at the door

or try to shut it," said Adelita. "I was in a hurry to find the backpack." Adelita took her cell phone out of her pocket. "I need to call Rick and then see Twila. I just hope that she has insurance for the missing necklace."

"What is insurance?" Benny asked.

"You buy insurance when you want something to be protected in case it is damaged, lost, or stolen," said Henry. "The insurance company will pay to replace or repair it as long as the damage or loss wasn't your fault."

"Insurance would cover the value of the missing necklace," agreed Adelita. "But it would not replace Twila's beautiful creation."

"Twila did say that she needed the money," said Jessie.

"I think she would rather have her necklace back," said Violet. "She was very upset to lose it. She said she didn't even want to sell it."

"That's interesting, Violet," said Adelita. "Rick and I were in her store recently. Twila seemed proud to show her creations, but when we asked about price, she'd change the subject. Rick wondered how she stayed in business!" Adelita pulled out her cell phone and punched numbers.

Henry remembered the cell phone call he had overheard Twila receive outside the hangar. Suddenly something didn't seem right about that call, but Henry couldn't put his finger on what it was.

"Rick isn't answering," said Adelita. "My car is down by the lake in the main parking lot. I'm going to head out. Thank you so much for your help." Adelita stooped to give Watch a big hug. "Especially you, my dear friend."

"Watch did have a little help," said Henry. He pulled out Adelita's glove and handed it to her. "I borrowed this from your hangar."

"Good idea!" said Adelita. "A search dog can track better if it has a scent to follow. Rick and I have transported SAR teams many times. We know quite a bit about it all."

Watch licked Adelita's face as if to say good-bye. The children also said good-bye and watched Adelita walk away.

"You're right, Jessie," said Henry. "Adelita

didn't steal anything."

"That's right," said Benny. "Watch would tell us if she did!"

The children followed Watch as he led them back through the woods.

"I agree," said Henry. "But I'm not so sure about Rick. He did work on the door, and the door came open, causing the backpack to fall out."

"But we know that he and Adelita are good friends," said Jessie. "Why would he get his friend in trouble?"

"That's a good question," said Henry. "We should talk to Rick again."

Just then Watch barked. He was back where he had found the backpack, pawing the leaves and wagging his tail.

"Now what did you find?" Jessie asked. The children gathered around Watch. They peered at something glinting in the leaves.

"I think Watch has found another treasure!" said Benny.

"Yes, he has," said Violet, picking up the object. "It's a silver earring, shaped like a

dragon! Do you think it came from the backpack?"

"Adelita said the backpack was zipped up tight when Twila put it into the baggage compartment," Jessie pointed out.

"But it was partly open when Watch found it," Violet said. "I have photos." Violet took her camera from her pocket and the others gathered around. They peered at the photos of the yellow backpack full of jewelry.

"I remember now," said Jessie. "The backpack was open about halfway when Watch found it."

"Somebody must have opened it after it fell from the airplane," Henry said. "Or else there would be jewelry scattered all over the place."

"This earring doesn't look like the other jewelry in the backpack," said Violet. "Look, you can see that all the jewelry in the backpack had pretty gems. And it was all made with gold, not silver." She showed more photos on her camera then held up the earring. "This earring is silver, and it has no gems. It's different from everything else that we saw in the backpack."

"I think we might have a very good clue," said Henry.

"I do too," said Jessie. "Whoever owns this earring might be the thief!"

Violet remembered something. "Jason wears a lot of jewelry," she said.

"And I watched him admire the jewelry in

the backpack," said Benny. "I remember him leaning over me to look at them. He said he also made jewelry."

"I noticed that he frowned when he talked about how he could not afford to have a store like Twila does," said Jessie. "Maybe he's jealous of her."

"Jason said he and Bounce were at the river when we saw someone in the woods," said Henry.

Violet thought of something else. "Jason also has a pierced ear but no earring," she said. She looked at her sister and brothers sadly. "Do you think this is Jason's earring? And he's the one who stole the necklace because he is jealous of Twila?"

"It would be terrible if a SAR member did something like that," said Jessie. "We need to talk to Jason."

CHAPTER 7

Dock Diving for Answers

"Hey," said Benny, "here come Marianella and Goyo!"

The children and Watch greeted the newcomers. The dogs pawed at each other and played like they'd been friends for years.

The children told Marianella about finding her sister Adelita and the backpack falling out of her airplane. Then they told her about Watch finding the silver earring.

"Wow, you have been busy!" said Marianella. "That is great news that Adelita is innocent!"

Violet looked down sadly.

"What's wrong, Violet?" asked Marianella.

"Actually, we wanted to talk to Jason," said Henry. "Is he coming back here too?"

"Jason took Bounce down to the lake to practice dock diving," said Marianella. "The lake is straight down that path." She pointed. "It's not very far. What's up?" Marianella looked at Violet but Violet looked away.

"We just want to talk to him," said Jessie.

"Okay then, let's go," said Marianella. She led the Aldens down the path to the lake. She looked back at Violet as she trailed behind her brothers and sister and wondered what was wrong. Watch walked at Violet's side and kept nudging at her hand.

* * *

"There's Jason," said Henry. "He's on the dock and Bounce is with him." The children walked to the dock and waved when Jason saw them. Bounce raced down the dock to greet Watch. They wagged their tails and sniffed each other.

"Dogs make friends so easily!" said Benny.

"And they remember their friends too," said Jason. "Nice to see you again, Benny. Are you here to teach Watch dock diving?"

Henry looked at Violet. She was staring at Jason's ear. "We wanted to ask you a question," said Henry. "It's about a..."

"It's about a dog that needs to learn how to dock dive!" blurted Violet. She smiled.

"Well, okay," said Jason, laughing. "Let Bounce and me show you. Come on, Jessie. Since you are Watch's handler, you should be the one to teach him."

Jessie shook her head at Violet, wondering why her sister hadn't asked Jason about the earring. She followed Jason and Bounce to the end of the dock. Watch was ahead of them all, barking and racing back and forth.

"Look at Watch," said Benny. "He's ready to dock dive!"

"He sure is," said Violet. "Jason will be a good teacher."

"Why didn't you want to ask Jason about the earring, Violet?" Henry asked.

Violet watched as Jason gave instructions

to Jessie. She smiled again. "Because I know it's not his," she said. "I remembered something!"

"Oh, I know!" said Benny. "I remember too!"

"What did you two remember?" Henry asked, smiling at his younger siblings.

"Jason likes only gold jewelry," said Benny.

"That's right," said Violet. "He wore only gold yesterday. And today, he has just gold on again. He's also wearing a gold and turquoise earring. I saw it just now."

"Hm," said Henry. "Maybe he wears silver sometimes. We could show him the dragon earring and see what he says."

"Okay," said Violet. "But I don't think that it's Jason's earring."

"Hey!" yelled Benny. "They're going to start!"

Henry, Violet, and Benny watched in wonder as Jessie yelled, "One, two, three... Go!"

Three things happened at once: Watch and Bounce raced toward the end of the dock

when Jessie let them go. Jason tossed a red rubber float toy into the water. Watch and Bounce leaped after it.

"Good dog, Watch!" Jessie yelled.

Watch swam to the floating toy and grabbed it before Bounce could get there. Then Watch turned and paddled back to the dock. Bounce splashed after him, barking happily.

Jessie hugged and petted her soaking wet dog when he climbed back onto the dock. She was proud of how Watch had caught on to dock diving so quickly. The rest of the Aldens joined them on the dock and cheered.

"That was terrific!" said Jason. "Watch caught on right away. Good job, Watch! You too, Jessie."

Henry and Violet looked at each other and Henry nodded.

"Jason, we have something to show you," said Violet. She pulled the silver dragon earring from her pocket. "Watch dug this up near the site where he found the yellow backpack."

"Wow," Jason said. He took the earring from Violet's hand and looked at it closely. "This is beautiful. Look at the fine detail. You can even see scales on the dragon's body." Jason turned the earring over in his hand. "This is handmade, using lost-wax casting."

"Lost what?" Benny asked.

"Lost wax," said Jason. "It's a process to make jewelry pieces like this. The artist creates the form out of wax. It is shaped and carved. Then the wax piece is set in a container and a mixture poured over it. The mixture hardens into a mold. Then the wax is burned away, or lost, in a hot kiln. The artist pours hot liquid metal, like gold or silver, into the mold. The metal takes the wax shape that was left behind."

"So the wax really is lost!" said Violet.

"That's right," said Jason. "And then replaced."

"Do you make lost-wax pieces like this one?" Violet asked. She loved the jewelry that Jason wore, especially the blue turquoise.

"Yes, I do, for other people, but I never

wear silver," said Jason. "I'm allergic to it! Plus, I really like gold." Jason studied the earring again. "You know, this piece looks like one of Twila's designs."

"But it was nothing like anything else we saw in the yellow backpack," Henry said. "Those pieces all had gems and were made of gold."

"Then the thief who stole the backpack must have lost this earring," said Jason.

"So, the thief was already a fan of Twila's Handcrafted Jewelry Creations," said Violet. "That's interesting."

"I think you have a clue," said Jason. "You just need to find the owner of this earring. Perhaps Twila will remember who she sold it—or the pair—to."

"Do you want me to take you back to her store?" asked Marianella.

"Sure," said Henry. "We'll see if she remembers."

"We also need to talk to Rick again," Jessie reminded her brother.

"That's right," said Henry. "We should

go there first if Marianella doesn't mind dropping us off at the airport."

"No problem," said Marianella.

"It sounds like you have a busy day ahead of you!" said Jason. "Come back anytime to practice more dock diving."

"We will," promised Benny. "And if it's warm enough, I'll dock dive too!"

CHAPTER 8

Things Are Sticky

Once at the airport, the Aldens looked for Rick. No one seemed to be around.

"He's probably in the office if he's here," said Henry. "But where is the office?"

"There," said Benny. "I see the sign on that big building," he added proudly. "It reads *office*."

"Thanks, Benny," said Henry. "Your reading is a very big help!"

They found Rick inside, sitting behind a desk piled high with papers and notebooks.

"Hey, Henry, Violet, Jessie, and Benny," he greeted them. "And you too, Watch. What can I do for you all today?"

"Watch found Adelita," said Jessie. "She was in the foothills, camping out and searching for the yellow backpack."

"I know," said Rick. "She called me a little while ago. She said she's coming here after she talks to Twila."

"You also saw her yesterday," said Henry quietly. He watched Rick, looking for a reaction.

Rick smiled. "You're right, I did see her," he said. "She was the person we saw from the air wearing the red jacket and waving."

"Why didn't you tell us?" asked Violet. "You knew that we were trying to find her so we could tell her we had the backpack."

"I told you Adelita wasn't a thief," said Rick. "And I still believe that. But I didn't want her to be found until I could talk to her. But I guess you found her without my help." Rick petted Watch, and Watch licked Rick's hand. "I know you were doing your job, Watch."

"Adelita told us about her broken baggage compartment door," said Jessie. "And that you fixed it for her."

"That's right, I did," said Rick. "What's that got to do with anything?"

Henry noticed that Rick was acting cross.

"The door flipped open and the backpack fell out," said Henry.

"No way!" said Rick. "I installed all new hardware and latches. That baggage door wouldn't flip open if it was locked properly."

"Could it be shut and not locked?" Violet asked.

"Nope," said Rick. "The door is designed to pop right open once the latch is unlocked."

"What if the door was stuck?" Benny asked. Then Benny told everyone about the sticky stuff he'd felt on the bottom of the baggage compartment opening.

"I have no idea what that could be," said Rick. "Let's check it out!"

They walked down the row of hangars to Adelita's plane. Benny felt the doorway again and showed them the light-green goo that stuck to his fingers.

"I wonder what it is," said Rick. "I didn't use anything like it when I installed the new parts. Let's see if the door sticks to it." He lowered the door so it touched the goo. The door didn't pop open.

"Would it stay shut even if the plane was flying?" Henry asked.

"There's only one way to find out," said Rick. "Let's take her for a spin!"

"Oh boy, another plane ride!" said Benny. Rick laughed and helped Benny climb into Adelita's plane. Henry followed close behind, excited about another chance to be Rick's copilot.

"Are you girls coming?" Rick asked, looking back.

"I think I'll skip it," said Violet, remembering the bumpy ride from the day before.

"I'll stay here with Violet and Watch," said Jessie. "We can see what happens from down here."

"That's a good idea," said Rick. "Here,

you can probably see better with these." He pulled a pair of small binoculars from his jacket pocket and handed them to her.

Jessie used the binoculars to watch as Adelita's plane taxied down the runway and took off. She and Violet took turns with the binoculars as the plane rose, circled Sunriver, and headed toward the foothills.

"Look, the door just popped open!" said Violet.

"I saw that. It took a while, didn't it?" said Jessie. She spied Adelita's plane as it circled around and headed back to the airport. She could see the door very clearly using the binoculars. "I guess Rick, Henry, and Benny saw the door pop open too," she said.

"Hey, who's got my plane?" said a voice. Jessie and Violet turned to see Adelita standing behind them, petting Watch. He was enjoying the attention. Jessie and Violet hadn't heard Adelita walk up behind them but Watch had.

"Rick took your plane for a test ride," said Jessie. "He's coming right back."

"I see him returning," said Adelita. "Are your brothers up there with him?"

"Yes," said Violet. "Benny and Henry love to fly! But I am happier to be here on the ground."

Adelita laughed. "You just have to get used to flying in a little plane," she said. The three watched as the plane landed and slowly taxied back to the hangar.

Rick opened the door and helped Benny out. Henry followed.

"Did you see what happened?" Benny asked. "The door stuck for a while, then it popped open."

"The door was rigged to come open during the flight," said Henry. "Somebody wanted the backpack to fall out."

"Wow," said Adelita. "Who would have done that?"

"Hello, Adelita," said Rick. "We're trying to solve your mystery. Benny noticed sticky goo on your door. We just found that the goo would hold the door shut even if the door was not latched."

"But Twila was the one who put the backpack inside the baggage compartment and shut the door," said Adelita. "Nobody else was around."

"Maybe Twila thought the door was locked," said Rick. "You would also think it was locked, Adelita. You didn't know about the goo that was making the door stick shut."

Henry thought of something. "But if someone rigged the door to open so the backpack would fall out, how would they know where it landed?" he asked.

Jessie recalled how easily she and Violet had seen the plane just now. "Maybe they used binoculars," she said.

"But they could only see where it fell out," said Henry. "How would they find where it landed?"

"The backpack was bright yellow," said Violet. "It would be easy to spot."

"It was a very clever plan," said Jessie. "And I guess it worked. But why would the thief take only the necklace?"

"Speaking of the missing necklace, I talked to Twila about that earlier," said Adelita. "I apologized and promised to keep looking for it. But Twila acted like it was no big deal."

"That is strange," said Violet. "Twila was very upset when she told us the necklace was missing. She said it was the best creation she ever made. It could not be replaced."

"That's right," said Adelita. "She told me the same thing when she showed it to me before she zipped it into the backpack. But today she said her insurance was going to cover it, and not to worry about it."

"We were going to talk to Twila next," said Violet. She showed Adelita and Rick the silver dragon earring and told them how Jason had said it looked like one of Twila's creations.

"If she remembers who bought it, we might have our thief," said Jessie.

"Hm," said Henry. "I just thought of something. Maybe Twila has already figured out who took it. That's why she isn't worried."

"I just thought of something too," said Benny.

"What is that?" asked Violet.

"We haven't had lunch yet!"

"That is true," said Jessie. "We can stop at the diner in the village before we see Twila."

"Oh, please join us for lunch," said Rick. "I've got all the makings for peanut butter and jelly sandwiches in the office. You do like P-B-and-J, right?"

"You bet!" said Benny.

Henry helped Rick put two tables together in the airport office while Jessie and Violet helped Adelita smear peanut butter and raspberry jelly on wheat bread. Benny found a large bag of corn chips in a cupboard. Rick brought out paper plates and napkins and opened cans of cold orange soda for everyone. Henry put water in a bowl for Watch, but Watch seemed more interested in the sandwiches and corn chips.

"You'll eat when we get home," said Jessie. "No more people food for you!"

Everyone sat down to eat lunch.

"How's this for a fancy spread?" Rick asked, smiling.

"It's just perfect," said Adelita. "As always."

Jessie noticed that Rick and Adelita kept exchanging looks and smiling. Were they hiding something? Were they really innocent?

The children thanked Rick and Adelita for lunch. Then they headed back to the village to talk to Twila. As they walked, they talked about the mystery.

"Did you see how Adelita and Rick kept looking at each other?" Jessie asked. "It's like they were sharing a secret."

"I still think they are both innocent," said Henry. "Rick seemed very surprised about how that baggage door was rigged."

"And Adelita would not have been in the woods searching if she was the thief," Jessie pointed out.

"And don't forget that she told the truth to Watch," Benny reminded everyone.

"Jason is also innocent," said Violet. "And he had a great idea."

"Yes, he did," agreed Henry. "Twila might know who the silver dragon earring belongs to. She would remember who she sold it to."

"And then we might know who the jewel thief is," said Jessie.

CHAPTER 9

Lost Wax

"Uh-oh," Jessie said when she saw the sign on the door to Twila's Handcrafted Jewelry Creations. Watch sniffed at the closed door and wagged his tail.

"What's wrong?" Benny asked. Benny studied the sign. "*Closed for lunch*," he read. "There's a clock too. It's set for two o'clock."

"You're right!" Henry said. He patted his little brother on the head. "So, Twila will be back at two o'clock. I guess we'll have to wait."

"Let's take Watch to the park across the street," said Violet. "We can have him search for things. Remember what Marianella said?"

"Yes," said Jessie. "Handlers and their dogs should always be in tip-top shape!"

The children crossed the street to the park.

Benny read the sign at the park entrance. "It says *dogs welcome*. I like this park!" he said.

They all took turns hiding sticks and encouraging Watch to locate them.

Watch suddenly looked across the street and barked.

"What is it, Watch?" Jessie asked.

Watched yipped again as a man carrying a briefcase walked out of Twila's Handcrafted Jewelry Creations.

"What's that man doing in there while Twila is at lunch?" Violet wondered. "And why does Watch care? Maybe we need to follow him and find out who he is."

Just then Twila came out of her store.

"Wow, she was inside all along," said Jessie. "Let's go talk to her."

"Wait," said Henry. "Twila is carrying something. Let's see what she is up to."

The children stood quietly and watched as Twila walked to the alley next to her store. She was carrying the yellow backpack.

"Look, she just tossed the backpack into the trash bin in the alley," said Jessie. "I wonder why. It was a nice backpack."

"She told me it could not be cleaned," said Violet. "She said she would never buy yellow because it showed dirt so much."

"Then why did she buy a yellow backpack to deliver the jewelry?" Jessie asked.

They watched as Twila walked back into her store.

"Let's go talk to that man," Henry said. "Maybe he knows something."

Jessie put Watch on his leash. The children headed across the street and caught up to the man with the briefcase.

"Hello," said Henry. "May we ask you a question?"

The man stopped and faced the children. Watch strained on his leash to sniff at the

man's briefcase. The man noticed and held the briefcase out for him. Watch sniffed it and wagged his tail.

"What do you smell, pal?" he asked. "It's just a bunch of boring insurance stuff." The man stooped to pet Watch. "You're a good dog, aren't you?" Then he stood up. "What would you like to know?" the man asked Henry.

"Oh, we just wondered if you know where the airport is," said Henry. He glanced at his brother and sisters. They stood and waited. They all trusted that Henry knew what he was doing.

"Sure," said the man. "It's just past the big park across the road. You can take a path to it. I think it's about a half mile from here."

"Thanks very much!" said Henry. "Have a nice day."

"Same to you," said the man. He gave Watch another pat on the head and continued on his way. The children watched as the man headed up the street.

"Henry, we know where the airport is,"

said Violet. "Why did you ask him that question?"

"Because Watch got the answer to our real question," said Henry. "What was the man doing in Twila's store?"

"I know!" said Benny. "He was her insurance man. He was giving her money for her missing necklace."

"Either that or getting the information," said Henry. "And Watch was very interested in the smell of that briefcase. Let's go in and talk to Twila now."

Jessie waited outside with Watch as the other Aldens entered Twila's Handcrafted Jewelry Creations. Twila was behind the counter at her worktable. She looked up as the bell jingled.

"Hello again!" Twila said, smiling. "You are just in time to learn something about making jewelry. Would you like me to show you?"

"Yes, that would be fun," said Benny. He noticed that Twila was much more cheerful than she had been before. She was carving something and humming when they walked in.

"I'm creating a jewelry piece from wax," said Twila. "But it will soon become solid silver."

"Lost-wax casting!" said Benny.

"That's exactly right," said Twila, looking surprised.

"We learned about it today," said Violet. "But we have never seen it done."

"How funny," said Twila. "Okay, I'll show you the first step for lost-wax casting. Benny, take this ball of wax and warm it with your hands. Then you can form it into any shape you like." Twila handed a small, light-green ball to Benny.

Benny gasped. Then he watched as Twila demonstrated how to warm it. He pressed the ball of wax between his hands. Then he twisted and worked the ball into a shape.

"It gets softer as it gets warm," Benny said. He looked at this brother and sister. They nodded their heads.

"That's right, Benny," said Twila. "See

how easy it is? My, it looks like you've made an interesting shape."

"It's a dinosaur," said Benny. He held up his green wax creation. It had a head, tail, and four stubby legs.

"That's very nice," said Violet. She looked at Henry.

"Very nice, Benny," said Henry.

"You have now made something for a lost-wax casting, Benny," said Twila. "I guess you already know what happens next." Twila turned to Henry and Violet. "So, what can I do for you children? Did you find my missing necklace? Not that it's a big deal anymore. My insurance is going to pay for it."

"We didn't find the missing necklace, but we did find something else," said Violet. She held up the silver dragon earring.

"Oh, this is very interesting," said Twila. She took the earring from Violet and peered at it.

"We thought that it might be one of your creations," said Jessie.

"Why, yes, it is," said Twila. "Where did you find it?

"It was close to where Watch found the yellow backpack," said Henry. "We think whoever bought this earring from you is the person who stole your necklace."

"Really!" said Twila. "That is also very interesting. The problem is, I can't remember who bought it. I don't even know if there was one earring or two." Twila laughed nervously. "Sometimes my memory just isn't what it used to be. Besides, I already know who the thief is. It is Adelita."

The children exchanged looks. They remained quiet. Twila talked faster.

"Adelita knew how valuable my necklace was because I told her. She must have set up the baggage compartment door to flip open. That door has sprung open before. I heard all about it. Then she disappeared and later you found her in the woods. It all makes sense. Adelita is the thief!"

Just then Twila's door burst open and Watch charged inside. Jessie was being dragged from behind, trying to hold him back. Watch broke free from Jessie and raced around the counter to where Twila was standing.

All the children tried to grab Watch as he sniffed at Twila's shoes and then her apron pocket. He ran circles around her, barking wildly.

"Watch, *no!*" Jessie yelled. "Come here!" Jessie ran to Watch and grabbed him by his collar. "I am so sorry!" she said. "Watch is usually very well behaved. I don't know what's wrong with him."

"Get that mutt out of my store, right now," said Twila. "The rest of you may leave with him."

The children apologized and left. They walked back to the park.

"Watch acts like that only when he's found something important," said Jessie. "He did the same thing when he found the backpack and the earring."

"And now he's found something else," said Violet.

"Or someone," said Henry.

"Do you mean Twila?" asked Jessie. "Why would Watch be interested in Twila?"

CHAPTER 10

A Party!

"Watch smelled something on Twila's shoes," said Violet.

"And something in her apron pocket!" said Benny.

"Twila also acted happy just now," said Henry. "Like she was happier to have the insurance money than her necklace. Just like Adelita said."

"Why would she no longer care about her necklace?" Violet wondered.

"Because...the necklace isn't missing," said Jessie.

Everyone gasped.

"So there is no thief?" asked Benny.

"There is a thief all right," said Jessie. "I think Twila is the thief. Or she pretended to be..."

"You're right, Jessie!" said Violet, "Remember the bright yellow backpack? Twila said she would never buy yellow, but she did this time. I think she knew that yellow would be easy to find in the woods."

"And what about the green wax she uses for lost-wax casting?" Benny asked. "You didn't get to see it, Jessie. It was sticky! It looked and felt like the green goo from Adelita's baggage compartment."

Henry was thoughtful for a moment. "Let's say Twila is the one who set it up so the airplane baggage door popped open. How would she know where to look for the yellow backpack?"

The children recalled that Rick circled his plane over Sunriver Village before he soared over the foothills. Rick told them that it was the usual route planes took from the little airport. Twila could have driven back to her store and watched the plane as it flew.

"Oh!" said Violet. "I just remembered something else. We saw binoculars by Twila's window!"

"Yes!" said Jessie. "The pair that Rick loaned us made it easy to watch the door of Adelita's plane today. Twila could have been watching the plane from her store. She would have a very good idea of where the backpack fell."

"And she would have no trouble finding it in the woods," said Violet. "She must have been wearing the dragon earring and dropped it when she ran."

"I just remembered something too," said Henry. "When Twila left the hangar yesterday, she received a phone call. I think it was her insurance agent."

"That's weird," said Jessie. "Twila had just discovered that her necklace was missing. Yet the insurance agent called her, she didn't call him."

"She was already scheming to get the money," said Henry.

"And keep her necklace too," said Violet.

"Wow," said Benny. "That's probably not right—to pretend something was stolen to get money for it."

"No, it is not right, Benny," said Henry. "I think we need to talk to Twila again."

The children went back across the street and walked boldly into Twila's Handcrafted Jewelry Creations. Twila popped up from behind the counter. Violet immediately noticed that she was wearing the silver dragon earring.

"What are you doing back in my store?" Twila yelled. "Get that dog out of here at once."

"We found your thief," said Henry. "And you know who it is."

"Yes, I do," Twila stammered. She looked nervous. "As I told you, it is Adelita! Why don't you believe me?"

"We think you rigged the door of Adelita's plane to come open," said Henry.

"What?" cried Twila. "Why on earth would I do that? And how? Adelita told me that the door had been fixed recently. I trusted her with my precious jewelry. I made sure the door was shut."

"It was not shut," said Jessie. "It was just stuck."

"Stuck with some of your green wax," said Benny. "Then it popped open in the air. The wax got soft and tur-bu-lence made it let go of the door." Benny looked proudly at his brother and sisters.

"And then you went to the foothills and found the bright yellow backpack," said Violet.

"That is ridiculous," said Twila. "How would I ever find it? It fell from a plane!"

"Why do you have binoculars?" Jessie asked. "Don't jewelers use magnifying glasses for their work?"

"I watch the birds at the park across the street," said Twila. "I like birds." She walked around to the front of the counter and pointed to the park. She fiddled with the silver dragon earring in her ear.

"We think you had another reason for

using binoculars," said Henry. "You watched where the backpack fell. Then you drove to the area and found it. It was you we saw running in the woods."

"And you took only the piece that you loved most," said Violet. "You couldn't stand to part with that necklace."

"But you needed the money," said Henry. "So you got both."

Suddenly Watch barked as the door jingled and the insurance man entered the store.

"So, we meet again!" the man said, bending down to pet Watch.

"I'm happy you came back, Mr. Gulbranson," said Twila, looking at the children. "I have something to tell you."

"And I have something for you," said Mr. Gulbranson. "I already have a check for your stolen necklace." He plunked his briefcase on the counter and snapped it open.

"Oh my," said Twila, "that was very fast!"

"I pulled some strings for one of my favorite customers," said Mr. Gulbranson. He handed a check to Twila.

"Thank you so much, Mr. Gulbranson," said Twila. "But I can't accept this money."

Twila handed the check back and reached into the pocket that Watch had been sniffing earlier. She pulled out a huge gold necklace. Bright bangles and colorful stones glimmered in the light from the front window. Violet's eyes opened wide.

"You see, there has been a big mistake. My precious necklace has been found!"

"Well! I am delighted that your treasure has been located," said Mr. Gulbranson. "I suppose my work here is done." He put the check back into his briefcase and snapped it shut.

"Thank you so much," said Twila. "These children were the ones who found my necklace, with help from their dog, Watch."

"Ah," said Mr. Gulbranson, who petted Watch again. "Excellent work, children, and you too, pal." He waved good-bye and headed out the door just as Rick and Adelita entered the store.

"Hey, everyone, what's up?" said Rick. The

children noticed that he and Adelita were holding hands.

"Hi, Rick! Hi, Adelita!" said Jessie. "We're so glad to see you. Twila has something to tell you both." Jessie smiled, finally realizing why Rick and Adelita had been looking at each other earlier. And why Rick had been so protective of his friend.

Twila explained what she had done. "I'm really sorry," she said. "I hope you can forgive me. I want to make it up to you both if I can."

"Maybe you can," said Rick. "You see, I just asked Adelita to marry me. Then I realized that I didn't have an engagement ring for her! We came here hoping to find something she would love."

"Rick has always been a little impulsive," said Adelita. She gave him a playful shove.

"I appreciate how you're willing to forgive me," said Twila. "And I think I have just the ring for you, Adelita."

Twila reached under the counter and brought out a small wooden box. Violet's eyes got wide again when Twila opened the box. Inside was a dazzling gold, ruby, and diamond ring.

"I created this many years ago and have never had the heart to sell it," said Twila. "It is one my best. I love it even more than the necklace." Twila handed the ring to Rick, who placed it on Adelita's ring finger.

"Perfect fit," sighed Violet.

"I think this ring has found its rightful owner," said Twila. "if you will accept it as my gift?"

"Oh my, yes," said Adelita.

"It's beautiful," said Rick. "Thank you so much. But Twila, I hope you've learned your lesson!"

"You bet I have," said Twila. "I learned that I can't outsmart a smart dog or four very wise children!" She laughed and gave Watch a pat on the head. "And I learned that I should be more honest in my business."

"We are very happy we could help you," said Jessie.

"You do make beautiful jewelry," said

Violet. Henry and Benny nodded.

"Thank you," said Twila. "And I need to learn to part with my creations if I want to make a living. This is a good start."

* * *

Saturday afternoon was the annual picnic for the local search-and-rescue dog teams. And it was Marianella's turn to host the event. On Friday evening, Henry and Jessie helped Victor and their grandfather prepare a huge meal. They made a big fish chowder with potatoes, carrots, and onions. They baked loaves of bread and chopped chunks of cantaloupe and pineapple. Jessie made dozens of homemade chocolate chip cookies.

Saturday morning Violet and Benny helped Marianella unfold tables and chairs. They set everything up in the backyard. Violet covered the tables with bright, colorful tablecloths while Benny set out the plates and utensils.

"Where will the dogs sit?" Benny asked.

"Don't worry about the dogs," said Marianella. "They will romp, chase, and take naps wherever they choose. It's a big yard!"

"I'll make sure there are bowls of water for them," said Benny.

It turned out to be a beautiful sunny afternoon in Sunriver. The Alden children greeted Rick, Adelita, and Jason. Jason introduced them to other SAR team members that joined the picnic. Soon the yard was full of people and dogs.

"One, two, three, four, five, six..." Benny counted. "Seven, eight, nine—wow! There are twelve dogs in the yard!"

"And they are all good friends," said Marianella. "Even if they just met, they know how to get along with one another."

"Dogs are smart about a lot of things," said Benny.

"It helps to have smart people around them," said Marianella. She nodded to all the Alden children. "You all did a great job solving the mystery."

"And it won't be their last," said Grandfather, chuckling. He hugged his grandchildren close. "I never know what mystery they will solve next!"

Everyone gathered at the food table and filled their bowls with fish chowder. They helped themselves to homemade bread and fresh fruit. It didn't take long for most of the food to disappear.

"I would like to propose a toast," said Jason. He stood up at his table and everyone became quiet. "To Rick and Adelita! May they have a happy life together—both on the ground and in the air!"

Everyone held up their drinks and shouted, "Hear, hear!"

Rick and Adelita stood up and smiled. Suddenly Bounce leapt up on Rick and almost knocked his drink out of his hand. Bounce barked happily and wagged his tail. Goyo and Watch started barking and soon the other dogs at the party joined in on the fun. Rick and Adelita plopped down on the grass and let the dogs lick and paw at them like they were part of their pack. Everyone laughed and clapped.

"It looks like the dogs also say, 'hear, hear!'" said Benny.

One stormy afternoon, the Aldens take a shortcut through the Greenfield Cemetery and wind up in the middle of a haunted mystery! Many in town believe it's good luck to leave a gift at the LaFonte family gravesite. But when bad things happen to people who don't leave gifts, the old legend seems like more than just superstition. Is the LaFonte ghost for real?

CHAPTER 1

In the Cemetery

"I think it's going to rain," twelve-year-old Jessie Alden told her younger brother, Benny. "We need to walk faster if we're going to beat the storm," she said. Jessie gently tugged on Watch's leash. The wire-haired terrier trotted between Benny and Jessie, keeping pace with their quick steps.

"I'm going as fast as I can," Benny replied. "The wind keeps pushing me backward."

He looked ahead toward his ten-year-old sister, Violet, and fourteen-year-old brother, Henry. Violet was struggling with the zipper on her jacket and Henry's hat kept flying away in the strong gusts.

"It's too cold," Henry complained as he swooped his hat off the ground for the fifth time and set it firmly over his short brown hair. "Taking Watch for a walk seemed like a good idea an hour ago—"

"It was warmer then," Violet responded with a shiver. Her two high pigtails whipped back in the wind. She gave up on the zipper and wrapped the jacket around her instead. "We should have stayed closer to home." Violet shoved her hands into her pockets.

"Nothing to do about it now," Jessie said as she and Benny caught up with their siblings.

Benny was breathing heavily. "This is crazy strong wind. If you tied a string to me, I'd be a six-year-old kite."

Jessie took Benny's hand in hers and squeezed it tight. "I'll make sure you don't blow away," she said, holding him firmly.

"I have an idea." Henry pointed to the nearby gate of the Greenfield Cemetery. "There's a shortcut this way."

"Shortcut?" Benny stared past the tall, ornate iron gate toward the moss-covered tombstones. "Sounds good to me. Let's go!" He rushed forward.

"Hang on." Jessie put a hand on Benny's shoulder. "Cemeteries are spooky." Jessie was very brave, but she was also cautious. "Are you *sure* it's okay with you, Benny?"

"I'm not a chicken." Benny put his hands on his hips. "I don't believe in ghosts."

"Once we get to Main Street, we can stop at a shop and call Grandfather for a ride," Henry told them.

"The quicker we get home, the faster we can eat!" At that, Benny's stomach rumbled. "My tummy says it's almost dinner time."

"It's only four o'clock," Henry told Benny after checking his watch.

"Hmmm." Benny pat his belly. "Feels like dinner time. My tummy needs a snack."

"You *always* need a snack!" Henry laughed.

Jessie looked to Violet. Violet often kept quiet about things. Jessie wanted to make sure Violet got a vote before they decided to go through the graveyard.

"Are you scared, Violet?" Jessie asked.

"A little," Violet admitted. "I don't know if I believe in ghosts or not. Sometimes I do. Sometimes I don't..." Violet's voice tapered off. "I suppose if everyone else wants to go that way, it's all right."

"Great!" Benny pushed open the gate. "We all agree. Come on."

Jessie held Watch's leash as they stepped onto the cobblestone path. The sky grew darker with each step they took. Violet moved close to Jessie.

Henry walked ahead with Benny. They were checking out the gravestones, taking turns reading the names and dates out loud.

Greenfield Cemetery was built on a hillside. The wind howled through a thick grove of trees planted in the oldest section. Tombstones in that part dated as far back as the late 1700s.

"There's a lot of history around us," Jessie remarked.

Benny pointed at a tombstone. He sounded out the engraved word. "Soldier."

"The soldier died in 1781. That means he probably fought in the American Revolution," Henry told Benny. "I'll read you a book about the war when we get to the house."

Jessie, Violet, Henry, and Benny lived with their grandfather. After their parents died, they ran away and hid in a railroad boxcar in the woods. They had heard that Grandfather Alden was mean. Even thought they'd never met him, they were afraid. But when he finally found the children, they discovered he wasn't mean at all. Now the children lived with him, and their boxcar was a clubhouse in the backyard.

Watch was the stray dog they'd found on their adventures.

As the first drops of rain began to fall in the cemetery, Watch barked toward a far-off building. It was along another stone pathway past the trees.

"Is that a house?" Benny asked, squinting his eyes. Drops of rain speckled his thick dark-brown hair.

"I think that's the main office," Henry replied, tilting his head to study a squat, brown building. "There's a sign out front. I can't read it, but there's also a parking lot. That's a good clue it's where Mrs. Radcliffe works."

Mrs. Radcliffe was the caretaker of the cemetery. The children had only met her once when they were out with Grandfather. Grandfather Alden had been born in Greenfield and knew practically everyone.

"You're looking the wrong way." Benny tugged on Henry's arm and pointed to the right. He asked again, "I meant is *that* a house?"

Not very far away, tucked among the gravestones, stood a stone structure, much taller than anything else. It was made of white marble, with carved columns and a triangle roof. The building looked like an ancient Greek temple. Several bouquets of white lilies were lying on the front steps.

"It's not a house," Jessie told Benny. "That's called a mausoleum."

"Maus-a-what?" Benny asked.

Violet began to explain. "It's a fancy kind of grave where—" She was about to tell Benny more, when suddenly, lightning flashed. In the glow, the children saw something move by the mausoleum. "Who's that?" Violet asked.

A shadowy figure emerged from behind the building. It was impossible to tell if it was a man or a woman. Whoever it was had on a black jacket with a hood and was moving fast around the tombstones.

The figure stopped and stood near the big mausoleum. An instant later, a flash of lightning zigzagged across the sky and the figure disappeared.

Watch snarled.

Benny stepped back and put a hand on Watch's head. "Watch is scared," he said, leaning in toward the dog. "He thinks we saw a ghost."

Jessie looked at the nervous expression on Benny's face and said, "We should get out of here."

There was a small wall around the back of the mausoleum. They could easily jump over it. Just past that was a café where they could warm up and wait for Grandfather.

Watch barked as the rain began to pour down in heavy sheets. Thunder rattled soon after the lightning.

As the children began to run, Henry glanced back over his shoulder. "Odd," he mumbled, staring at the spot where the cloaked figure had disappeared. "Something strange is going on in Greenfield Cemetery."

THE BOXCAR CHILDREN SPOOKTACULAR SPECIAL

created by Gertrude Chandler Warner

Three spooky stories in one big book!

From ghosts to zombies to a haunting in their very own backyard, the Boxcar Children have plenty of spooktacular adventures in these three exciting mysteries.

978-0-8075-7605-2
US $9.99 paperback

THE ZOMBIE PROJECT
The story about the Winding River zombie is just an old legend. But Benny sees a strange figure lurching through the woods and thinks the zombie could be real!

THE MYSTERY OF THE HAUNTED BOXCAR
One night the Aldens see a mysterious light shining inside the boxcar where they once lived. Soon they discover spooky new clues to the old train car's past!

THE PUMPKIN HEAD MYSTERY
Every year the Aldens help out with the fun at a pumpkin farm. Can they find out why a ghost with a jack-o'-lantern head is haunting the hayrides?

THE BOXCAR CHILDREN BEGINNING

by Patricia MacLachlan

Before they were the Boxcar Children, Henry, Jessie, Violet, and Benny Alden lived with their parents on Fair Meadow Farm.

978-0-8075-6617-6
US $5.99 paperback

Although times are hard, they're happy—"the best family of all," Mama likes to say. And when a traveling family needs shelter from a winter storm, the Aldens help, and make new friends. But the spring and summer bring events that will change all their lives forever.

Newbery Award-winning author Patricia MacLachlan tells a wonderfully moving story of the Alden children's origins.

* * *

"Fans will enjoy this picture of life 'before.'"—*Publishers Weekly*

"An approachable lead-in that serves to fill in the background both for confirmed fans and readers new to the series." —*Kirkus Reviews*

GERTRUDE CHANDLER WARNER discovered when she was teaching that many readers who like an exciting story could find no books that were both easy and fun to read. She decided to try to meet this need, and her first book, *The Boxcar Children*, quickly proved she had succeeded.

Miss Warner drew on her own experiences to write the mystery. As a child she spent hours watching trains go by on the tracks opposite her family home. She often dreamed about what it would be like to set up housekeeping in a caboose or freight car—the situation the Alden children find themselves in.

While the mystery element is central to each of Miss Warner's books, she never thought of them as strictly juvenile mysteries. She liked to stress the Aldens' independence and resourcefulness and their solid New England devotion to using up and making do. The Aldens go about most of their adventures with as little adult supervision as possible—something else that delights young readers.

Miss Warner lived in Putnam, Connecticut, until her death in 1979. During her lifetime, she received hundreds of letters from girls and boys telling her how much they liked her books.